A CLOUD DOES NOT KNOW WHY
IT MOVES IN JUST SUCH A DIRECTION
AND AT SUCH A SPEED,

IT FEELS AN IMPULSION --- THIS
IS THE PLACE TO GO NOW.

BUT THE SKY KNOWS THE REASONS
AND THE PATTERNS BEHIND ALL CLOUDS,
AND YOU WILL KNOW, TOO, WHEN
YOU LIFT YOURSELF HIGH ENOUGH
TO SEE BEYOND HORIZONS.

HAPPY HOLIDAYS,
STEVE

Winds Across the Sky

A Love Story

Chris Foster

with drawings by Pam Holloway

Aslan Publishing
PO Box 108
Lower Lake, CA 95457

Published by
Aslan Publishing
P.O. Box 108
Lower Lake, CA 95457
(707) 995-1861

For a free catalog of our other titles,
or to order more copies of this book
please call (800) 275-2606

Library of Congress Cataloging-in-Publication Data:

Foster , Chris, 1932
    Winds across the sky : a love story / by Chris Foster. -- 1st ed
        p. cm.
    ISBN 0-944031-43-9 (casebound) : $12.95
    I. Title.
PR9199.3.F573W56   1992
813' .54--dc20

                                                91-39977
                                                CIP

Copyright © 1992, Chris Foster

Cover illustration by Anthony Casay
used by permission of artist and Casay Gallery.
Cover design by Scott Lamorte and Brenda Plowman.
Book design by Brenda Plowman.
Interior illustrations by Pam Holloway.

Printed in USA
First Edition

10 9 8 7 6 5 4 3 2 1

For Joy and Durwin

Acknowledgements

I give special thanks for the contribution which my wife and friend, Joy, now departed, made to the initiation and completion of this book. I wish to thank Pam Holloway for her drawings—a labor of love; Dr. John Ford, of the Vancouver Aquarium, who so cheerfully shared his knowledge of whales; the helpful people at the Vancouver Public Library in British Columbia; my good friends and "mentors" in the writing and publishing business, David Walmark and Richard Baltzell; my publishers, Dawson Church and Brenda Plowman; and the friends with whom I live in spiritual community. I especially thank my father, Reginald "Fireman" Foster, a reporter for fifty years in London's "Fleet St.," who started me in my writing career.

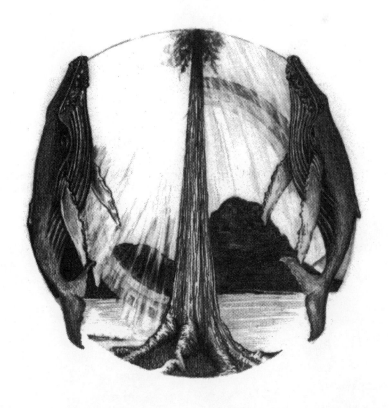

Sometimes I go about pitying myself,
and all the time I am being carried on
great winds across the sky.

—*Ojibway saying*
adapted by Robert Bly
from the translations of Frances Densmore

❧ Prologue ❧

It was a playground for gods, and indeed these were gods who disported themselves with such gleeful abandon off the wild sea coast.

The wind, gusting at up to thirty miles an hour, had created a swell which as far as the eye could see was spattered with flying foam and scud as the gusts tore at the water's surface.

The group of southern right whales entered the bay at noon and within twenty minutes were pursuing their play with a passion that rivalled the passion of the wind. A mature bull began the game, flipping his body downward toward the vertical while at the same time hoisting his tail high above the water into the hot breath of the gale.

With his flukes unfurled proudly like a spinnaker and presenting a sail area of nearly seventy square feet the bull—joined swiftly by the others—began "sailing" to the far side of the bay. He stopped only when he was in danger of beaching, when he would turn and swim back to his starting point and begin again.

There were fifteen whales in the pod. Although full of enthusiasm, the younger ones often had difficulty finding the proper set for their tails. They caught the wind for a short while but then lost their coordination, at which point, either from exuberance or impatience, they would bring their flukes down with a thunderous slap upon the waves and try again. The whales played for nearly two hours before settling in for a nap. Finally the bull turned his snout to the north and the rights resumed their migration from the Antarctic to warm waters off the coast of Brazil, where they would devote the winter to the pleasurable work of mating and calving.

We are creatures of the sea and creatures of the air and there was a time, long ago, when we were your friends, when love arched between us as a rainbow and we communed and played together as we served the god of earth and heaven, the god of sea and sky, the god of circles. Then you turned, and in your turning, turned against us. Still you hunt us down and maim and kill. Is it merely for profit that you carry out such destruction? Or in some dark corner of the soul are you jealous of creatures who do not toil, as you toil, or suffer, as you suffer, but are happy simply to honor life's ancient ways—to live and to be—to frolic, to feed, and to love one another?

As you are at home in the earth, we are at home in the sea. As you have your mountains and plains and cities so too do we, but our mountains are the crashing waves, our plains are the broad reaches of oceans, our cities are the towering palaces of ice that greet us each year at the poles.

We are large, yes. Perhaps it is because we are so large that you began to see us as monsters, as beasts to be feared. Yet we are large only because the sea is large, and the distances we must cover are large... and because the circle we must draw between the sea and sky is large.

We have the same beginnings as you. When we lie gestating in our mother's womb, when we, like you, are weak and small and helpless, we are surrounded by the same water. We too have red blood in our veins. We too breathe and shout, talk and sing and dance.

We are still your friends despite the horror and pain you have brought upon us, and as the barriers dissolve we tremble at your touch.

1

In the warm Pacific waters off the coast of Mexico a female humpback whale with a distinctive, starlike cluster of barnacles on her chin had discovered a plank floating upon the sea.

The plank had entered the humpback's field of vision as she swam at the surface with her newborn calf. The mother whale had spent the past nine or ten weeks alternately resting and feeding her young one; finally hunger urged her to begin the long migration north to her summer feeding grounds in the Gulf of Alaska.

Despite the hunger chafing her body the whale was too intrigued by the ten-foot long timber to pass it by. At first she simply butted it a few times with her head, getting a feel of its weight and composition, investigating what kind of object it was. As realization developed that the plank was "neutral" yet responsive to her initiatives, the humpback began to explore other ways of interacting with it. Soon she was swimming in lazy circles around the flotsam, from time to time changing direction and—with a sudden increase of speed—swimming directly at it like a predator charging its prey. At the last moment she would dive, passing beneath the plank with pinpoint precision and surfacing on the other side.

The young male calf watched his mother's play with increasing excitement. At last the calf—three months old and already weighing four-and-a-half tons—could be a spectator no longer. He charged the plank himself. But his timing was wrong and he collided heavily with the flotsam as he tried to dive beneath it. His next two attempts were no better, but the fourth time he barely scraped his back as he glided under the plank. Soon, to his mother's approval, he too could perform the maneuver flawlessly. It was hard work, of course. Though his mother now wanted to resume the journey north her calf insisted—with urgent nudges and cries—upon being fed. The mother turned on her side under the water, her breast nearly exposed at the surface. The calf, lying parallel to her and with his head pointing in the same direction, clutched greedily at a teat, holding it between his tongue and palate. He sucked the powerful squirts of thick, creamy milk so eagerly that it surprised his mother, who knew he had gorged himself five times already that day.

The harsh throb of a destroyer's engines hurt the ears of the whales but the din faded as they swam steadily north, diving and spouting in unison. Late in the afternoon they met a group of spinner dolphins, who gambolled and leaped almost directly in their path and kept them company for a while. They also met a large group of sperm whales—a mixed nursery school of mothers, juveniles, and calves. The shy sperms, after a curious look at the humpbacks, backed off and continued on their way.

The sun was setting on the horizon's rim when the agonizing noise of a large cruise ship reverberated through the ocean depths. But from deep within the jarring cacophony of sound, the sensitive ears of the mother whale distinguished a faint tone that sent a thrill of pleasure shooting through her. It was the exuberant grunts and chatter of more humpbacks traveling in the same direction as she was, but further out to sea. She responded immediately, calling out with her own distinctive cry, and altered course to join the others. Before long there were seven humpbacks—including two calves—blowing, breathing, and diving as they moved rhythmically, majestically in a line northward, feeling the water grow gradually cooler, feeling the promise of abundance to come, noting with pleasure the increasing density of plankton in the sea.

The plankton meant there would be lots of nice fat fish and krill when the time came to dine in Alaskan waters.

2

The giant redwood grew beside a creek about ten miles in from the sea, where it was sheltered from coastal winds.

There was a special bond between the tree and the ocean, embodied by the soft mist that rolled in from the sea each morning and nourished the patriarch with water. Each day the needle-like leaves of the redwood combed the mists for moisture. Each day, as the fog burned off, the needles were bejewelled with beads that sparkled and glinted in the sun.

For twenty-seven hundred years the tree had been sending its shallow roots probing and digging into the fertile soil of the flat, so that today the roots covered an area of nearly two acres.

For twenty-seven hundred years the tree had been reaching up to the sun, until now, at a height of three-hundred-and-forty feet, it dwarfed the Californian landscape.

The redwood was a survivor of an ancient kingdom that has now been virtually destroyed. But once those hushed dark red chambers contained a greater abundance—in terms of total weight of plant life—than any of the forests of the world.

The tree's first love was for the sun, because it was the sun that gave it power and energy, indeed, which was the source of its very existence. But the redwood loved the earth also—and with just about as much passion.

The tree gave shelter to plants and animals—to the purple-hued oxalis and other gaily-colored wildflowers that bloomed on the forest floor; to families of deer and squirrel; to butterflies, ferns, and the darting humming-bird.

The tree manufactured food, that the miracle of life might continue.

It helped to check erosion and regulate climate and each time it breathed it belched out huge clouds of oxygen to replenish the atmosphere. Because of its critical contribution to all forms of life in the forest the redwood provided a context for the vast and intricate ecosystem of which it was a part.

The tree was a bridge between earth and sky, and up and down that bridge in constant motion flowed all the riches of these two worlds, the dark world beneath the surface of the soil, invisible yet teeming with life, and the light world above where there is rain and wind and vastness and where clouds fly high and the sun shines in its strength.

The tree helped to bind the forces of light and dark, that they might dance together.

Because of the redwood's presence, the forest was a place of music. A place of harmony. A sacred place in which birds, insects, plants , and all other living things joined together in a song of praise to life.

3

The movie actress with the dancing brown eyes and vivacious smile was flying home to California from Canada. As she flew on metal wings through the night the woman was thinking about the time she had just spent with her mother. The thoughts whirred through the actress's mind as rapidly as frames in a movie.

How beautiful she still is, that dark-eyed woman with the strain of Gypsy blood who brought me into the world, but also how unsettling. Yes, she nodded and smiled politely as I told her my news, the new house in Hollywood, the friends, how it went in the last movie, and the new part that I'm hoping to get. But admit it, Monique. She touched a raw nerve.

"Are you happy, ma chère?"

Remember how she waited so patiently—waited until you had run out of words—before she asked the question? And remember how quiet it was, just the noise of the old grandfather clock, daddy's favorite, going tic-tac as it has for two or three hundred years. Funny to think it was ticking away before either of us were born. Why did I feel so threatened, as if I had to try to defend myself? I used to hate that clock, but there was something reassuring about it in that moment. I suppose it was saying that at least one thing in life is dependable—time itself—ticking away in the hall of our home in Montreal.

What a question to ask though, and so suddenly, out of the blue.

"Are you happy, ma chère?"

What did she want me to say, this extraordinary woman, who in her earlier years wounded the hearts of half the handsome and eligible bachelors in Europe? You used to be so active, maman, such a social person, before father died. Now it's as if you've found a private garden somewhere inside yourself and have retreated into it. Is that why I made this trip home, to touch your serenity? If it was, it didn't work. I feel more confused and vulnerable than ever. "Are you happy?"

Who even knows what happiness is? Yet your question keeps haunting me. Thank you for being gentle, though, and not making an issue of it. I know we would have had a fight if you had.

Bon dieu, I'm starting to cry. Thank goodness everyone is sleeping. You do not understand, maman. To win the kind of movies and parts I want I have to make sacrifices. My work has to come first—and you did agree it has opened doors I could never have dreamed of. This is my talent. This is what I can do. I love acting. I bring pleasure to millions of people. I have a responsibility to give it everything I have. ... Perhaps some people can afford to go and search for truth, to find a private garden inside themselves, but I have to keep my mind on my job. I have to meet the continual challenge of competition and deadlines and yet, and yet ... your question tugs at my heart.

Don't be so silly, Monique. Pull yourself together, and go to sleep. Of course you're happy. How could you not be? You may not have a man—not at the moment, anyway—but you've got everything else that counts—money, fame, some wonderful friends. What more could you want?

Maudite! Merde! The question will not go away. Perhaps another drink will help me to sleep. "Stewardess, some more champagne please." Too strong the pull of this strange life I lead, that others see as glamorous, though God knows the glamour is thin enough at times.

"How do you know, maman?" That is what I should have asked her. "How do you know when you are happy?"

4

"Trouble always comes in threes," the man thought to himself bitterly as he walked, unsteady, a little hesitant, into the spare room he had fixed up as a study.

His wife had left him six months ago. His father had passed away three days earlier at the nursing home. And now the dream had come back—the nightmare that had tormented him many years previously when he returned home from Vietnam.

The man was a reporter and a would-be novelist, and he had gone to Vietnam at the age of twenty. The image in his dream was always the same. He was leading his platoon across the paddies to Hill 4 when the Vietnamese began blasting away from their hiding places. He brought his rifle to his shoulder and was contributing to the noise and savagery when he saw one of the enemy rise up and run over a bare patch of ground toward a comrade. It was the first time he had killed someone. A voice inside him was saying, "You can't do this—look, he's a medic, he's trying to help," but in the heat and excitement of the moment he fired at the running figure anyway. The medic fell, riven by bullets. Then he arose, blood flowing down his shattered chest, and began walking toward the young American lieutenant. His arms were outstretched. There was a shy yet eager smile on his face. "Please, let us be friends," the man kept saying as he advanced. The whole

19

platoon was firing at him now and the noise was deafening. But the Vietnamese kept coming, arms outstretched, smiling.... Finally his body vanished in the hail of bullets and there was only his face and arms. The face kept coming closer though, with the same shy but eager smile. It came to within a few feet of the American and one of the hands reached out as if to touch him. "Please, let us be friends," said the face one last time. The smile vanished and a single huge tear formed on the medic's cheek before everything blurred.

The man sat down at his desk. His body slumped and his chin dropped close to his chest.

What kind of retribution was this? What kind of justice? He thought the dream had vanished, had been laid to rest; for Christ's sake, he thought that he had succeeded in forgiving himself. Now he knew the shame had not really gone. It was still there, and this time it was going to win.

How still the house was without Jennifer. The man opened a drawer. He looked at the revolver which he had brought back as a souvenir from the war. He had been so young when he went to Vietnam, he thought to himself. So innocent. Like many others of his age, he had been torn between two conflicting views—the war was wrong, he was sure of that. But was it not also wrong to manipulate his friends and connections, to use privilege so as to avoid the draft and be safe and comfortable?

An even more pressing dilemma to be answered now, though, he thought dully. Was there any point to his life? Was there any reason to prolong his existence?

"I don't think so," he told himself. He thought of his failed marriage. He thought of his father, and how even in death the two of them had been unable to connect. The waves of grief and shame buffeted him without remorse and he reached out and picked up the gun he had brought home from Nam. There were bullets in a cardboard carton and he took one and inserted it into the chamber.

A heavy rain lashed the roof but the man did not hear. He raised the weapon. He held it for a few moments in front of him, looking at it.

"It is time," he thought, as his sense of purpose and meaning flickered like a dying candle and went out. "Time to go to that same dark, empty hell where I sent the Vietnamese medic."

 **5**

The humpbacks slept upon the gently rolling surface of the Pacific. Their tails stroked placidly up and down, just enough to keep their breathing holes above water. Occasionally one of the group would accidentally slip below the surface, but when this happened it would spout, take a breath, and resume its slumber as if unaware that anything had happened.

The whales slept, at peace, while within their cavernous forms, encoded in their cells, filed safely in the vaults of their memories, slept the story of the ages.

Keepers of the record they are, these gentle beings, their ancient eyes a witness to the dawn of history. Before human civilization was born these graceful creatures cruised the green depths and communed with the sky and sun. As cataclysms and floods ravaged the earth and human empires rose and fell the whales continued about their honorable tasks, filling the ocean with the sounds of love and play, and with their dignity and strength.

* * *

The pirate whaling ship had once been a Japanese trawler, but had gone through a series of devious transformations, including changes of name. She was not registered as a whaler, of course, but as a fishing boat; besides operating under a dummy company she also flew a flag of convenience. The captain and crew were on their way home when they made their lucky find.

The carnage, when in their sleepy state the humpbacks were discovered by the killer-factory ship, was swift and efficient. The sea, that under the summer sun had shone blue and silver, turned the color of blood, and the stench of the dead and dying fouled the atmosphere for hundreds of yards around.

Only two escaped the terror of the harpoons, the adult female with the starlike cluster of barnacles on her chin, and her calf. So strongly did the mother swim in her flight that her calf was unable to keep up, but snuggled on top of her, positioning himself just below and beside her dorsal fin where the drag upon his body was less, and where he was able to increase his own speed.

After an hour the mother stopped to rest and to comfort the young humpback, holding him with one of her huge white flippers while he shuddered and cried, caressing him, calling to him, rubbing his body, his head, his immature flippers. But while she could comfort her calf she could not comfort herself. As she began to swim again, her calf a little off to one side now, the female humpback continuously sent out her moans and cries, telling of her anguish and pain. But there was no response from any of her kind. It was as if she were the only whale left in the sea.

The calf did not know what was happening but he knew his mother was distressed, and made his own little moans as they continued their solitary way north, some two hundred miles off the Pacific coast of North America.

6

All was ready for life's gentle but passionate miracle.

Water had been drawn up in a single flutelike column from the roots far below; since the branches of the redwood began more than a hundred feet above the forest floor, the water molecules had sometimes traveled 400 feet or more to reach the topmost needles.

Carbon dioxide had been gathered in from the clear blue atmosphere.

Like a king of old entering the chamber of his beloved, the sun entered the flat, taper-ended leaves of the redwood and the clusters of chlorophyll that had waited for that coming stirred and came alive. They quivered with power. They split apart the glistening molecules of water so that water's ancient forces of oxygen and hydrogen might be loosed.

From the interplay of fire and water and carbon dioxide was created food, in the form of simple carbohydrates, that life might continue on the planet.

So quiet was the huge tree in its operation. It sucked up more than a ton of water to its leaves every day, while performing hundreds of other important tasks, yet with all this busyness it made not a sound.

Day after day, week after week, year after year, it went about its work of blending the two realms, the realm of earth and the realm of light, but the only sounds were those made by the wind, when it blew in from the sea or from the northeast and stirred the high branches; or by the squirrel, as she ran chattering from one spot to another; or by the woodpecker, as he dug his sharp, curved claws into the thick bark of the trunk and began rapping his beak against the wood in quest of his supper.

Perhaps it was because the redwood was so quiet that it was able to hear the voice of the whale crying out from the sea.

"I hear you, my sister of the deep," exclaimed the redwood, hastening to answer the whale's cry.

"Remember that you are not alone in this ordeal. The actions of the humans were terrible, inexplicable. The same kind of terror happens here in the forests. We feel the harsh bite of their steel, the even greater pain of their blindness and indifference—and yet the lord of all life knows us, hears our ache, knows our enduring.

"I have stood in this spot for many hundreds of years. I was alive—a sapling full of youth and energy—when as a young man the Buddha left his father's palace and found wisdom and comfort beneath the bodhi tree.

"I was alive when the teacher Jesus was born and when the prophet Muhammad climbed to the top of Mount Hira. I was a king of the forest long before William the Conqueror defeated the British, or Columbus discovered America.

"For over two thousand years I have blended the forces of light and dark and brought peace into the earth.

"Yes, your friends and loved ones have been slaughtered, but in the dance of life we are one, you and I. Let me be your friend until you find others of your kind. Let us join together in communion.

"Can you hear me, great whale, in your home in the rolling waters?"

The female humpback lay motionless upon her belly in the sunlit sea, her barnacled back just about awash, listening to the redwood. She was virtually oblivious to the brattish behavior of her calf, who had been trying every trick he knew to get her attention—wriggling up onto her back, covering her blowholes with his body, even sliding down into the water off her tail. Finally the calf gave up his pestering and went to sleep, resting his head comfortably on his mother's broad back, the rest of his body supported by the ocean.

The words of the redwood warmed the humpback's heart and she knew a sense of comfort.

"Thank you for your words, my redwood friend," the whale replied.

"I feel your love and it gives me strength. My mother used to tell me legends and stories of a time when all creatures, including humans, were one, and lived at peace. She also told me stories about you and your kind. You are round, I believe, as we are round, and obviously you are very large also.

"Yes, yes, redwood. Let us be friends and commune together."

7

The sweet smell of the forest and the quietness were a balm to the man. He was reminded of the time he visited these woods with his father nearly twenty years before.

They had driven out in his father's old grey Studebaker and sat in the same spot where he was sitting now, at the base of a large redwood his dad said was nearly three thousand years old and over three hundred feet high.

"Funny to think the tree has been growing here ever since then," the man thought as he shifted his back against the trunk to make himself more comfortable. He remembered how his father told him stories about the war, like when he was shot down over France and was taken in by a farmer until it was safe to make a run for it. He had never felt so close to his father before—and never felt as close again.

"What happened to you dad?" the man thought angrily, remembering how his father gradually retreated into himself, relying more and more on drink, getting more and more feeble and helpless. "What happened to you? Where did the fire go?"

All of a sudden the man knew why he hadn't been able to pull the trigger a few days before. No matter what happened to him he couldn't just quit the way his father had.

What was it he was reading recently? Don't try to deny your feelings. However unpleasant they may be, let them come to the surface where they can be seen, and acknowledged. It's the only way to release them, the author said— if you try to suppress what you are feeling it will fester and turn into poison inside.

"It's true," the man thought. "I must let the feelings come up and not be ashamed. What I am feeling is a natural and normal reaction." Did he really believe that? He wanted to, sweet Jesus he wanted to.

But the author was wrong about god, the man decided. A god of love would not let a man rot and die the way his father died. A god of love would not let someone who was once a strong and capable guy get into such a state in the first place. There was no meaning to life when it ended that way—when the promise of youth dissolved into an aching void of nothingness.

"Careful, John," the man said to himself. "Take a deep breath. Try to relax."

But the waves of anger and pain kept coming. It was just like when he got back from Nam, the man thought, and everything was swirling around in his head and he couldn't make sense of anything. He felt the old, terrifying fear that he had taken a wrong turning somewhere in his life and it was too late to get back on the right track.

"Is it true?" he asked himself.

"Is it really too late? What was it Eliot called them? Hollow Men? Dear god, how could I end up so hollow? I've met a lot of failures and frauds, but still most people seem to get by with normal, happy lives. Or do they? Maybe it's all a sham. Hollow men and hollow women."

Without thinking, the man touched the bark of the tree. It was good to rub the spongy bark and feel its softness. It made the tree seem closer. "Be still for a moment," the man told himself. "Just let everything go."

How quiet it was. He had never known such quietness. He looked up at the redwood towering high above him into infinity. He thought of the constancy that had kept the tree upright and strong, giving of itself for so many hundreds of years, defying storm, fire, flood, and other natural disasters. He sighed, and without warning began to sob. With both hands holding his head John Bratton cried as he had never cried since his childhood.

8

In the darkness below the surface of the soil the root tip stopped probing and prying for a moment as it felt its way barred by a piece of rock. A little oil oozed over the protective cap that shielded the head of the tip in its journeyings. Thinner than a piece of string and perhaps an inch long, the root tip began to veer to the left, seeing if it could work its way around the obstacle. Again it ran into stone. It changed direction to the right. Soon it was making good progress once more, pushing through the soil with a corkscrew thrust as it sought out moisture and nutrients for transmission up into the body of the tree.

The redwood was aware of the presence of the man. It felt his sense of desolation. It felt his shame.

The huge tree was aware of everything that came into its field of force, large or small, and in its own way, at its own level of being, sought always to comfort, to blend, to give.

It felt the touch of the man who sat on the ground and ran his hand over the ridges and fissures sculptured into the redwood's skin.

The tree was a king, with a king's authority. Everything in the forest was affected by its radiance. Because he was in the redwood's electromagnetic field the man could not help but be influenced. The power and innate intelligence of the tree washed through him even though that expression of authority was inaudible to the human ear. The redwood directed its energies to the task of communicating with the man. Borne upon its pulsations of love was a message:

"You think you are alone, my human friend, but this is not true. Be still for a few moments. Sense my presence. Hear the song of the All That Is. It sounds within you and all around you in every tree and plant, in the rippling murmur of the creek, in the soft sigh of the wind.

"May I tell you a little story? Large as I am, I would be nothing without the tiny rootlets that burrow beneath the surface of the soil and bring the water that I need. Sometimes as they search and pry they run against a stone or rock. That is what has happened to you. You have come up against a rock, and do not know what to do. But my little rootlets, when they run into the rock, veer to the left or to the right and soon they find an opening. They come into clear soil again. It is the pull of water that makes this possible—the roots come clear because the most important thing for them is to find that water.

"The water is like truth, my human brother. I am able to live and grow and stand upright because I see the truth of the great whole. This is what I love. This is what sustains me, and draws me on.

"Are you not also part of the music of earth and sky? Are you not also one with the wind and stars … with your own purpose to fulfill?"

9

This was one of the woman's most favorite places. She always felt good when she came into her kitchen and picked up a knife or pot and went to work. It helped to dissolve some of the stress that accompanied her work—the dark side of her huge dramatic gift.

Sun shone brightly through the skylight and windows as the woman stepped lightly into the kitchen on long limbs that could still make men turn their heads or forget what they were going to say. She put on a favorite apron. It was a riot of red and chartreuse that she had bought in Marrakesh while she was filming "Seeds of Desire."

The clock said two. She had made an elegant gateau aux poires before lunch and was now going to prepare the main part of the evening meal. It was unfortunate that her maid had taken sick, the woman thought to herself. But on the other hand she had wanted to make this a very personal offering.

The evening was important. A mutual acquaintance was bringing a well-known producer who—according to the grapevine—was looking for someone to play the lead role in a controversial new movie.

It was a role the woman had long coveted. When she learned the producer loved French cuisine she decided to invite him to her home so that she could display her culinary skills and cultivate his friendship.

The meal would comprise an hors d'oeuvre of coquilles Saint Jacques, salad Nicoise, and—one of her specialties—a main dish of coq-au-vin. It would be gracious and gourmet but not, of course, gaudy.

The woman had inherited her love of cooking from her mother. She saw the preparation of food as both an art and a ceremony—something like lovemaking!—that allowed her to express her refined, tender essences. She loved the feel and shape of a carrot. The aroma of fresh basil. The sharpness of a good French knife.

Yet on this particular afternoon, as she began cutting up the chicken she had bought at Giovanni's market, the woman was painfully aware that the intense currents of frustration and anxiety which had plagued her in recent months were still present. They had not miraculously dissolved as she entered the kitchen and began reaching for herbs and utensils. If anything, the turmoil she was feeling was worse than ever.

She felt an awful, indefinable dread.

Alone, with no one to see, the woman shook her head with frustration as she finished rubbing the pieces of chicken with garlic. Soon they would be ready for the quick dip into the frying pan that would sear the surface layers and lock in the juices.

Did the stress she was feeling have anything to do with the fact that she had passed forty and it was widely rumored that a younger actress—virtually an unknown in Hollywood, though she had made some successful movies in Europe—was being considered for the part that she wanted?

"Merde. Maudite." The woman swore under her breath as she set the frying pan aside and concentrated on preparing the sauce. While reaching for some ingredients she knocked over a mug of coffee that was sitting on the counter beside the stove. She swore again, more loudly. She had met the sultry Italian actress once at a party and been intensely irritated by her smug arrogance, the unspoken message: "I'm really much better than you. You're getting past it, you know."

Would the producer be tempted and choose the Italian peasant girl instead?

"I need the part. I really need it," the woman thought to herself. "I'm sick and tired of these ridiculous stories that say my career is going downhill."

The alarm clock emitted a cheery beep. 4:30 PM. It was time to get ready. Monique Dumont put the coq-au-vin into the oven and hurried from the kitchen, unaware of the small frown tightening her face as she tried to suppress her feelings of anxiety and foreboding.

❦ **10** ❦

The man sat down in his study and picked up his writer's journal. It was the secret place where he doodled and spent idle moments. In these spiral-bound pages he communed with himself and life, and nourished his passion to be a writer. With his cat dozing at his elbow, and an occasional sip of coffee to keep his brain in gear, the man wrote as follows:

May 10th:

Life will never be the same, and neither will I. I want to write about what happened yesterday while it is still fresh.

It may be that I touched the divine. I believe I did. I've read about such things but having it happen to me is something else, especially since I'm an unbeliever. I've never been so excited or happy in my life, although a nagging voice keeps trying to tell me it was just an hallucination—like what happened sometimes after I returned from Nam.

It wasn't an hallucination, though.

Start at the beginning—always a good idea. I was sitting down by this tree where dad and I sat and talked twenty years ago. The king of the grove, he called it. I was sitting by the base of this tree feeling like hell and thinking about the emptiness of my life when I sensed I wasn't alone. There was someone else near.

I'm good at this sort of thing even if it is a long time since I was in Nam—I looked around carefully but couldn't see a soul. It was weird. Then I realized it was the tree I was feeling.

That's how strong the PRESENCE of this tree was. The next thing I knew I started to cry. I've never cried like that since I was a kid. I wanted to in the war, god knows, but it never happened.

The tears kept coming and when they stopped the anger and fear and pain were all gone. I felt rested and at peace, at one with everything around me, particularly the redwood. I didn't just see a big tree any more. It was like I had been communing with a living BEING that has outlived thousands of years of human suffering and death and is still unmoved and at peace today. I had a feeling the tree had invited me into its own center.

You let me share your strength. I FELT the constancy in you.

What about that light I saw? Was it imagination? I know damn well it wasn't my imagination. Let's get it down, John. How would you describe it?

It was bright and intense and yet very soft. The trees glowed almost like they were on fire—but it all felt very peaceful.

I don't know how long the light lasted. A few seconds? A few minutes? I remember I looked at my hands and they were glowing too. I could see the streams of energy moving through them. I saw a bird and it was a shimmering little ball of light darting through the air.

I think that was when I shut my eyes, after I saw the bird. Maybe I was afraid I was going crazy. When I opened them again everything was normal. The light was gone, and the trees were just trees.

I kept thinking to myself, "Is this what I am really made of—light?" It was like I had been given a glimpse into the mystery of life and I had a feeling I would never be quite the same again. I held the tree for a few moments and walked away.

I guess I won't be able to talk much about what happened. They would think I was a real flake, wouldn't they, in the newsroom? But that's okay. It's okay. I know what happened.

What was it Shakespeare said? How did you put it, you wise old bird?

"There are more things in heaven and earth, Horatio, than are dreamt of in your philosophy...."

The man put down his pen. He felt satisfied. He picked up his empty coffee mug and went out to the kitchen, followed by a hopeful cat.

11

The woman with the dancing brown eyes finished putting her make-up on and checked her nails. She looked with satisfaction in the mirror at her emerald evening dress.

She hurried back to the kitchen. She took the elegant new apron with the delicate abstract design and tied it round her waist.

5:45PM. She was a little behind.

She checked the chicken and took a look at the radishes that she had put into iced water to curl. She reached for the biggest of her French knives and felt the edge. The blade was quite sharp but she honed it some more anyway and began cutting the carrots she had washed and left sitting in a bowl on the counter.

It was delicate work. The woman held the carrots in place with her left hand. With the point of the knife anchored on the cutting board she lifted the handle of the knife up and down in a practiced motion, slicing each orange cylinder into long, thin strips. She had performed the task many times. After they had been cut the strips would be glazed and arranged carefully on individual plates.

But this Saturday evening, as the aroma of coq-au-vin wafted through the kitchen, the woman's mind was not on the familiar ritual.

Her mind was like a sentry who daydreams at his post and fails to hear the rustling in the woods that spells danger.

Her mind was busy whipping up a storm cloud of resentment.

How long have I known Julia? Eight years? Ten? The best of friends we've been. So how come when I tried to tell her about these awful feelings I'm having she seemed to lose interest so soon? What's a friend for if she isn't there when you need her, willing to listen? When she had a hard time of it a year ago and went through that messy divorce I was there for her. I took her for walks, listened to her grief and pain. But when I tried to get into these deeper questions that are bothering me so much she just turned off. She didn't want to have anything to do with it.

There was no warning. The woman was slicing the last of the carrots when the knife slipped and sheered a quarter-of-an-inch into her thumb.

She let out a wail as she stared at the knife and at the blood seeping from the wound. Soon the blood was flowing faster. What a thing to happen. How deep had it gone? Her hands shook as she dropped the knife and lunged for a teatowel. She wrapped it frantically about her thumb. Her mind, so rudely awakened, was close to panic as it tried to focus on first aid and at the same time grapple with the implications of the accident.

"Mon dieu, only an hour before the guests arrive," the woman thought.

She felt weak; would she be able to finish on schedule? "Be calm," she told herself. "You must be calm. Everything is going to be alright." She sat down for a few moments, breathing deeply. Presently she washed the wound and put a bandage on it.

She completed the preparations in time but the accident was an omen of worse to come.

Impatient and angry with herself, she found more and more things going wrong. The confusion that had troubled her in recent months clung like a shroud, imprisoning her in its musty folds so that she could not do anything right. She spilt wine on the damask tablecloth. She made a joke that was off-key and ill-timed. Hurrying to fetch water from the kitchen, she tripped and nearly fell.

In a different context—if it had been an informal evening and she had been with close friends—it could all have been handled with a good laugh. But it was not that kind of evening.

After the producer and the others had departed, doing their best to hide their embarrassment, the woman shut the front door and leaned back against it. Tears poured down her cheeks.

But there was no release in the tears. They carried away none of her confusion or fear. They came from a place of emptiness, and as they slowly dried, emptiness was all they left behind.

The woman was afraid to even think about that emptiness inside her.

12

The trauma of the massacre was still a deep dark pain in the whale's heart. But as she swam with the others on the traditional migration route north the female humpback was aware of another memory seeking to assert itself in her consciousness.

It was a memory of human kindness.

When she was young, about four years old, she once became trapped in a fisherman's net west of Vancouver Island. Unable to get free, she was lying helpless on the ocean surface when the fishing boat captain and one of his crew came to investigate.

She heard a voice, a warm, kindly voice, as she focussed her left eye upon the two men and their boat. The man kept speaking to her in his soft, friendly way—as if he were speaking to a horse, and indeed he had been a rancher before he took to the sea.

She felt the calm in the man's voice. Although fear jumped through her the first time he touched her, the fear turned to a strange delight as she realized he did not mean to harm her, but that his spirit was gentle.

The man kept patting and stroking her as his crewman cut with his knife at the ropes that bound her. One by one the ropes were freed. If she had wished the whale could have crushed the tiny boat with a sweep of her tail, but the message was clearly imprinted in her brain that these men were friendly. She waited quietly until she felt the last of the ropes release their grip, and was careful as she dived and swam away not to swamp the boat that the men were in.

The two memories danced together upon the screen of the whale's mind: the terrible cruelty of the whalers; the care and compassion of the men who had freed her. For no special reason, she felt an urge to breach.

No hint the ocean gave that such a tumultuous event was about to occur; that beneath the surface of the sea a forty-ton humpback with a starlike cluster of barnacles on her chin was tearing along like an express train, propelling herself horizontally at top speed.

Suddenly she lifted her head and straightened out her tail. Horizontal propulsion converted to vertical thrust. The whale shot out of the water like a rocket. Straight up she leapt into the air and sunshine, her flippers grabbing and twirling, foam billowing from her warm, glistening body as she half-turned and landed with a practiced, thoroughly satisfying crash upon her back.

The ocean shook.

In the same instant a much smaller humpback also burst from the water in a similar maneuver. The calf was not as smooth or as skilled as his mother; he performed creditably, though. Just at the last instant, as he was trying to copy his mother and land on his back, he collapsed in a slightly awkward sprawl.

"The lord of all life is very good," the female humpback thought to herself, "who gives my calf and I the power to leap and dance and swim upon the blue ocean." She hugged her calf with an immense creamy white flipper so he would know he had done well.

"Did you hear me leap, redwood?" the whale called out a few moments later. "I wish you could be here so that we could play together. "

13

The great lord alights from his chariot and his form is clothed with mystery and majesty while his eyes shine with the splendor of a hundred thousand suns.

He is the lord of life and within him flow rivers and seas and within him soar eagles and mountains and cities and within him are contained planets and star systems and the mystery of the whole throbbing universe.

His consort accompanies him and there is not a single human being or any other form of life on the planet that is not included in her gaze and in her love. They come that all creation may share the radiance of their union. They come that all may be one.

They come to dance!

In one hand the great lord holds a little drum that goes tick, tick, tick; it is the drum of time, shutting out the knowledge of eternity.

In another hand, though, is a flame. For those who will let it happen, who will not flinch or draw back, the flame burns away the veil of time. It dissolves the barriers of separation. It opens the mind to eternity.

It brings tranquility and peace, a sense of immortal being resplendent within mortal flesh, untrammeled and free forever.

In the god's hair is a skull—death; but also a new moon—rebirth.

Lord of creation and destruction he is.

Lord of change.

Lord of the dance.

Upon bejewelled feet he whirls and his consort is with him and birth and death are with him. For how can something new be made unless there is the material to make it; and where will the material come from if not from old forms and structures that have served their purpose.

He dances that creation may continue and life's music resound. Yet the great lord, as he dances, is calm. His countenance is serene. No matter how passionate the dance, he remains at peace—birthless, deathless, and changeless, as it has been written, forever.

On the vast African plain, bleached and yellow in the hot sun, an old male wildebeest hears the tick of the little drum grow louder. The bull senses his time has come. He knows he can no longer keep up with the herd. Quietly he stops and turns, and alone, with massive dignity, confronts the stalking leopards.

In an oak tree in upper New York State, near the Canadian border, the monarch butterflies that had rested for the night at the forest's edge likewise hear the rhythm and music of the dance. It is time to fly south. Winter is coming. The monarchs pump blood into their wings to stretch them. They wait, ready to fly. A breeze steals through the branches of the oak—just right. The butterflies rise, a magenta cloud borne upon gossamer wings, and begin their long flight south.

All life hears the sound of the little drum in the god's hand that goes tick, tick, tick.

All life feels the heat of the flame that burns away the veil of separation and brings freedom.

≈ 14 ≈

The humpback whale was in a meditative mood and said to the redwood presently:

"There is something I have been thinking about, my redwood friend, and would like to discuss with you, because it puzzles me. Why is it that humans are so contradictory? Sometimes they act wantonly and cruelly, and sometimes a love comes through them that is so strong and radiant it uplifts everything around them.

"Consider how for hundreds of years they have been hunting us down without mercy, constantly refining their methods of destruction. Yet a few years ago when some whales became imprisoned in the Arctic ice—they had lingered too long at their feeding, as we do on occasion—the whole world wanted to help, and those who have been our worst persecutors became rescuers.

"This is a very strange situation. You have lived much longer than I, redwood. How do you explain it?"

The redwood had been noting with pleasure the cluster of toadstools that had shot up as if by magic from the rotting surface of a nearby log. The log had been down for nearly three hundred years but was still feeding essential minerals and nutrients into the soil of the forest.

"This is not an easy question," the redwood replied at length, "but here is what I think.

"My feeling is that humankind is easily distracted. Sometimes they hear the song of life sounding in their hearts, and something wonderful happens. They are wise, and caring. But then feelings of fear and isolation rise up and they think they must be aggressive and exploit the world around them in order to survive."

The whale lifted her flukes into the air preparatory to diving. Her calf followed suit, his movements perfectly synchronized with those of his mother.

"But there have always been some, haven't there, redwood, who hold true to that call of life," the whale exclaimed.

"Of course," said the redwood. "And I believe their numbers are increasing. Why, just the other day a man came and sat beside me and we shared a beautiful experience of communion together.

"It may be that while humans face enormous challenges in these days, this is all to the good. It may help open their eyes and hearts more fully to the song of the All That Is, so that they remember their true responsibility to the earth.

"I dare to think that humans are learning humility, and genuinely wish to understand us and come close to us...." The redwood stopped speaking for a moment as an eagle circled overhead and alighted on a high branch.

The whale, who had been listening intently, took advantage of the pause. She spoke up excitedly.

"This is why we must continue in our own expression of the truth we know, isn't it," said the whale, "so that we can help humankind? Just because we do not have hands or feet does not mean that we do not have a vital part to play in what is happening.

"My mother used to say that whales have a duty to keep love in their hearts no matter what human beings do. She said that in the beginning we were given the task of supporting the world—of being its foundation. If we were faithful in this then one day humans would have a change of heart, and all Nature would be safe at last."

The whale watched out of one eye as a small flock of terns appeared and began quartering the ocean not far from the migrating humpbacks.

The terns were flying only a few feet above the waves. When they sighted a fish they hovered for a brief instant and then plunged vertically into the water on long pointed wings, their tail feathers streaming behind them. They were voluble birds and screamed with excitement when they made a catch.

The humpback had a flash of inspiration. She knew what it was—the compulsion that had been stirring in her heart over the past weeks.

She forgot about the terns.

"Your words have helped me to understand something," said the whale.

"I have been feeling a tug in my heart which is new and strange. I am familiar with the usual urges of my kind—to feed, to mate, to bear young ones—but this is different. It is as if I am remembering something from long, long ago, and in some ways it is frightening, particularly when I think of the cruel attack by the whalers.

"Yet part of me is excited too. I feel an urge to draw close to humankind—to try to help dissolve this veil of separation that has kept us apart. Does this make any sense, redwood? Or is it an awful foolishness that is coming over me?"

The redwood spoke tenderly as the softest breeze.

"Of course it is not foolish," said the tree. "It is the most natural urge in the world.

"Human beings are rightly our friends. I support you in your compulsion, my sister of the deep.

"I sense you have an important mission to fulfill. It may be difficult—perhaps even frightening at times, as you say—but I will be with you."

15

"It was a good story," the man thought as he relaxed before his TV at the end of a long day. "A damn good one."

He had worked hard at the story for three days, giving it his best despite an occasional grouse from the city desk. He had seen a lot of duplicity and self-serving, in Vietnam and since becoming a reporter, so it had been refreshing to observe James Thompson's honest, giving spirit. The older black man had lost a good job with an engineering firm. After being unemployed and angry for six month he hit upon an original idea to build free vegetable gardens for poor people in the city. He'd been getting some support for his project, but not as much as he could have used.

At first when the reporter met Thompson he had been lukewarm about the story—a bit prejudiced, perhaps, he had to admit. But as the association developed and they began to interact more closely, a bond developed that cut through the barrier of race.

The reporter had been able to help the black man find new sources of free material and equipment. One day he also helped him build some planter boxes. It rained a couple of times, turning everything to mud, but they had worked on anyway; getting a hand on a hammer and pounding nails was the most satisfying thing the reporter had done for a long time.

As they unloaded the truckload of two-by-eights and
two-by-twos that they had scrounged, and cut the lumber
to size for the frames, and sometimes joked and cussed,
the two men talked about their wars, although not too
much. Thompson hadn't been in Nam but he served in
Korea. He had driven a tank there for a year until he got
shot up and burned.

The comradeship between the two went beyond
words. Often they had worked in silence, happy just to be
in one another's company, doing something useful and
practical and enjoying the genuine and sometimes teary-
eyed gratitude of the elderly people and misfits whom
they helped.

"There are a lot of ordinary people doing heroic things
that the world never hears about," the reporter mused as
he finished his beer in front of the TV and scratched his cat
in her favorite place under the chin.

Well, this time the world had got to hear about some
simple, everyday heroism, even though it was a shame
that the story was cut down at the last minute because of
other news—specifically, because of a rumored liaison
between the mayor and a local TV announcer.

As he cracked open a second beer and poured Amelia
some milk the man thought once again, as he had a number of times already, that a month or more ago he would
have been mad as hell at what happened to his story. He
would have complained angrily to the city editor. He
would have nursed the hurt in his heart. Some bitterness

did rise up alright, but it did not take command as it used to do.

Something else had welled up inside him that was more important.

"What Jim and I shared will outlive any story in a newspaper," the reporter said to the cat. She merely finished the last drops of her milk and—whiskers dripping—looked up imperiously for more.

No question about it, his life had changed dramatically since he visited the redwood, the man thought. It was so much simpler and more satisfying. There were not so many things to fuss about.

Was this how it was for the redwood, he wondered, as it kept reaching toward the sun and sky, as it kept probing with its roots for moisture.

≈ 16 ≈

The unhappy thoughts turned over and over in the woman's mind like a Ferris wheel in an amusement park.

What is happening to me? Why do I feel so frightened? Where is my joie de vivre? I used to be able to handle life so easily, now the smallest thing can make me explode. Even in the kitchen, my special place, I am afraid, and it is difficult to concentrate on what I am doing. It is all I can do to look after myself, and I'm not even doing a good job at that.

You've got to pull yourself together, Monique. Interesting … this trouble all started when mother asked me that stupid question, "Are you happy, ma chère?" What the hell right does she have to poke her nose into my life and my affairs?

I can't bear to think of yesterday. Merde. Merde. Why did I get so excited? How could I pull a trick like that on Victor? I know he likes to use a lot of master shots and keep the close-ups to a minimum. Why did it matter to me so much? I thought I was over that one years ago. He was perfectly justified asking for another retake, too; as directors go, he's a dear, everyone knows that.

I'm losing my grip and I don't know how to get it back. I only know I'm becoming a bitch. Just look at yourself, Monique. You've been shouting at your friends—not just poor Victor—you've been spilling coffee, bumping into people, breaking things. Your face is a disaster because of all the stress you're under ...

If only there was someone I could feel safe with and could talk to. The shrink is doing his best but he doesn't really understand what is going on and neither do my friends. If they talk to me at all now they just tell me not to worry so much, they say I've got a hang-up about Lia Marelli and there's no chance she will get the part I want. But it's not just Lia. There is something deeper and it is tearing me apart.

Where does it come from, this awful fear that there is a catastrophe coming? It's like I'm afraid I am going to lose myself.

What is happening, maman? I must write to you. No, that would be stupid, you will just try to take over and coddle me like you did when I was a child. Besides, I don't want to get you worried.

I hope I didn't overdo it yesterday on the set. Victor is a nice guy but he's no pushover. If he decides he has had enough—poof—he may refuse to work with me. It happened to Judy James and she was so sure she was indispensable. She thought she could behave any way she wanted and people would understand and forgive...then one day without any warning she got the chop.

What a strange life it is. Only a year ago the article in *Vanity Fair* said what a great actress I am and how intelligent and beautiful still. It was as nice a piece as anyone could hope for ... now look at me ... I think I am going crazy. I don't know if I can handle another scene like yesterday, with me shouting and swearing—mon dieu, where did I get such words?—and people trying to calm me down, and Victor walking away with a face like a thundercloud.

Do other people run into something like this where they're afraid they're going crazy? I've got to take more time for myself, that's all there is to it. I'm too stressed out. I'm a walking time bomb waiting to explode.

But I can't slow down. How can I? Not with the picture three months behind and everyone screaming. I wish it were worth all the hassle. I've got to hang in there and get a grip on myself. Other people cope when they run into real trouble, why can't I? Thank goodness for the new pills. If they help me through these awful days it will be worth it even if it does go against everything father used to tell me.

But you're not here, mon père, and I am. It's up to me. Courage, Monique, you'll get out of this. You've just got to get a grip on yourself. Stop worrying so much. Once you get this wretched picture finished you can take a long holiday—Tahiti, perhaps, or Thailand—remember how Meryl raved about Phuket the other night?

That's all that is wrong. Yes. I'm a little burned out. I need a good holiday … somewhere far far away.

17

The humpback was made for the joy of swimming.

For all her massive bulk she moved through the green depths like a ballerina, causing barely a ripple.

It is not so with the ships that human beings build. Rigid, inanimate things, they are always in a struggle with the element into which they are placed. They have to bludgeon their way through the water. Naturally the sea resists, setting up huge eddies and disturbances that slow a ship's progress.

The whale was a poem in motion.

She was a stream of light flowing through the larger stream of the ocean.

She was a song the creator liked to sing at sea.

She was one with the element in which she lived and moved, celebrating the beauty of her life.

The humpback glided through the ocean with a smooth, graceful, up-and-down motion, flexing the powerful muscles in her back and tail and achieving, as a scientist would say, "almost complete laminar flow."

Her skin was a miracle of technology by any standard, able to adjust instantly to changes of external pressure. It was constantly remolding and reshaping itself so as to prevent eddies from forming.

The glorious tail, twelve feet wide, with broad, deeply notched flukes, swept rhythmically against the water, also smoothing out turbulence as it alternated upstrokes and downstrokes. The humpback's great flippers—scalloped on their edges like cumulus clouds, ranging in color from black to snow-white, and measuring nearly one-third the length of her body—acted as stabilizers and helped her to brake and steer.

The ocean recognized its own. It streamed over the whale's exquisite body in a smooth flow, murmuring and chuckling and whispering endearments as it did so.

The humpback whale was not only made for swimming, of course. In the languid, pleasantly black depths of her mind, she was also a dreamer.

A born dreamer.

The redwood enjoyed this particular aspect of the whale's nature. In fact one afternoon the tree said to the whale:

"You know, whale, I am glad there is something dark and mysterious about you. You make me want to think new thoughts and have new imaginings. You make me remember things that I had never thought about before. You make me realize that there is always something new to be dreamed into existence. I like this effect you have on me."

The whale was sunning herself at the surface of the sea. "Thank you for your words," said the whale. "It is true, we are a dreamy lot in some ways."

There was a pleasurable silence between the two for a while before the whale spoke again:

"No more of this emotional nonsense I've been going through," she said to herself.

"I've finished that awful movie and soon I'll go on my holiday."

An interesting thought occurred to her. She decided to speak with Angelo later in the afternoon and accept the hunk's invitation to take her to a cabaret. He was an instructor at her gym. He had been eyeing her and they had been chatting frequently of late.

"It will do me good to let my hair down," the actress thought happily. "It feels like a long time."

The woman's hands, tanned, slim, with long, sensitive fingers, guided the steering wheel. Her feet, clad in an old pair of favorite blue runners, performed the familiar tasks of accelerating and braking the car.

The collision came without warning. She had stopped at a major intersection and was starting to pull ahead when it happened. She simply didn't see the red Corvette. It had been speeding down the main thoroughfare and tried to whip past the crossing on a stale light.

A very stale light.

There was a terrible grind and a crash of flying metal and glass.

Fear jolted through the woman, releasing a flood of adrenalin.

The Corvette had rammed the front right-hand side of her car. She watched, as if it was in slow motion, while her automobile slewed wildly in a 360-degree turn, locked in an embrace with the Corvette. She saw the driver of the other car. She saw his young, handsome face frozen in horror. She was certain she was going to die.

The awful crashing and grinding continued, and then suddenly—as suddenly as the collision itself—the woman did not care any more. She was floating about six feet above her car, and there were people gathering all around. She saw a man wrench open the door on the driver's side and peer inside. Soon an ambulance came. She watched as two attendants gently lifted her clear of the car and laid her on a stretcher.

She could see that her face was white and there was blood all over her. She could see that her eyes were closed. The people who were standing around looked shocked and worried and she wondered why, because she knew she was fine. She didn't hear any words, but she knew what the two men who were treating her were saying.

"Let's get a move on," one of them said. "She looks real shocky—get some high flow oxygen on her right away."

She watched the attendants lift her into the ambulance and close the rear doors. She tried to tell them that everything was all right, but they did not hear her.

The ambulance drove off. She knew her body was in the ambulance. Again she tried to say that everything was all right. It was at that point, when she realized no one could hear her, that she knew she was dead.

Immediately she was in a tunnel with a bright light at the end. The tunnel seemed to go up and up; it was whirling in a spiral and she knew that the light was god.

She was being drawn closer to the shimmering light at the end of the tunnel. The light was warm and comforting. She felt utterly at peace. There were two people in the tunnel with her, helping her. She knew what they were saying even though they didn't use words. They told her she was safe, and they would take her into the light. She couldn't see their faces—they were just shapes in the tunnel—but she could feel the love coming from them.

She came out on the other side of the tunnel and it was like being in a garden filled with flowers and light; there were colors she had never even seen before. It was incredibly beautiful, but then she saw the being who was the source of the light, and she forgot her surroundings. She felt completely loved and nourished. It was the most wonderful moment she had ever known. She told the being about the accident. She said that if it was possible, she would like to stay in the garden. But the being told her there was still important work for her to do in her earthlife. It made her happy when she heard that, so that she felt ready to return.

There was no sense of time. As she relaxed in the presence of the being she saw her whole life pass before her, as if on a movie screen. She felt all the emotions that had been present at different times in her life—her own emotions, and also the emotions of others. She realized how everything that had happened to her was actually connected.

She saw not only large events, but small ones too. She saw the scene in which she took away her sister's favorite doll out of spite. She felt her sister's pain, her feeling of loss and betrayal. She relived the moment when she went to the aid of a boy who was being taunted by bullies; she felt the relief that filled the small boy's chest as he ran away; she felt the pain that assaulted her when one of the bullies struck her in the face.

She saw the time when she blew up hysterically at her mother and father, telling them that she hated them, and they did not own her life, and she was damn well going to Hollywood whether they liked it or not. She felt their pain and grief—their inability to communicate, or to understand.

It was as if nothing could be hidden. She saw the repercussions of everything that she had done. In the presence of the light there were no excuses. Yet there was no shame in the revelations, either. There was just a magnificent sense of freedom. As the review unfolded she *was* the people she had hurt. She *was* the people she had helped. The review finished. The being of light said, "It is time to go back now." Again there were no words. She just knew what the being was thinking. The love that she felt for the being was different from anything she had known on earth.

She went back through the tunnel and woke up in the hospital where two doctors were working on her. They were saying, "Monique, Monique." She saw her body lying on the operating table. She knew the doctors were worried. She tried to tell them that she was going to be fine, but they did not hear. She saw one doctor put paddles on her chest and she saw her body bounce up.

When she awoke, Monique Dumont tried to tell the doctor she saw him put the paddles on her chest, but no one wanted to listen.

The first thing she saw when she looked around the room was a vase of yellow chrysanthemums on the table beside the hospital bed. She burst into tears. She realized she had never really seen a flower until she came back from the dead.

She touched one of the flowers and she knew the flower was part of her, and she was part of the flower. She knew the universe was alive. She knew it was all one.

ONE...

When the doctor came in again a little later he smiled reassuringly and said she had been unconscious for five hours. He had a nice smile. He told her that while she was unconscious they didn't know whether she was going to live or die. She had been very lucky, the doctor said. She had lost a lot of blood and had suffered lacerations and a broken collarbone. But her internal injuries did not appear to be serious, and he expected a full recovery.

The woman was back in the familiar world. She thanked the doctor. After he had left she gazed at the bouquet of flowers beside her and thought to herself, "This is amazing. Here I am in serious condition in hospital. My holiday is off. It will be months before I'm well, and very likely I won't get the part I was hoping for. But right now none of it seems to matter. None of it matters at all."

Later, some friends came in to see her—including her agent and some studio executives. She saw the concern back of their smiles and reassured them as best she could. But what she really wanted to do was to tell them about the miracle that had happened. She wanted to describe the tunnel, and the radiant being who had enveloped her in such total, all-forgiving love. She wanted to tell them about the magnificent calm that had swept through her soul. She wanted to say that they too would be welcomed into a realm of light when they died, and have opportunity to review everything they had done in their lives.

But she knew she could not do any of those things. Her friends would not understand.

She would have to keep her experience to herself.

She stretched, luxuriating in the glow of tranquility that filled every particle of her being. She knew that what she was feeling came from a place deep in the core of her soul—and not merely from the pills the nurses were giving her.

❦ 19 ❦

The three-thousand mile journey was over.

It was time for the feast.

Joy—huge, fierce, unrestrained joy—swept through the small pod of cavorting humpbacks as they reached their destination, the place where they would begin their summer feeding: the cold waters of the Gulf of Alaska, where all manner of tasty delicacies awaited their pleasure.

Some of the whales had lost more than a third of their total body weight during their winter stay in the warm waters off the coast of Mexico. But that situation would soon be rectified.

The group entered the sheltered waters of Icy Bay, in sight of Mount Saint Elias and the Malaspina Glacier, at noon, gorging deliciously on schools of fish and upon the krill which bloom in polar waters. Sometimes the shoals of shrimplike crustaceans were so abundant they turned the sea reddish-brown for miles around.

Below the surface of the sea the humpbacks lunged, and lunged again, scooping food into their mouths. Excited seabirds wheeled and dived for handouts as the whales catapulted to the surface, mouths agape. Shutting their jaws, they expelled the seawater through their sieve-like mat of baleen bristles; the fish and krill that remained made an enormous movable feast.

Several of the humpbacks used a sophisticated feeding technique perfected by their species over hundreds and thousands of years. Fifty feet or so underwater, they began swimming in an upward spiral, while at the same time forcing bursts of air through their blowholes. The escaping bubbles rose in vertical streams to the surface, creating a "net" within which krill and small fish were easily taken. The size of the net could be varied. So could the size of the bubbles, which the humpbacks adjusted to suit the dimensions of their catch.

The feasting continued.

The adult female with the starlike cluster of barnacles on her chin lunged, and scooped, making a thorough glutton of herself. At the same time, of course, she was teaching her calf all she knew about dining in polar waters.

She was able to satisfy her urge for food, but there was another urge in the humpback that was not being satisfied.

It was the strange, unfamiliar compulsion she had talked about with the redwood—the urge to draw close to humans, and commune with them.

The compulsion was growing inside her as strongly and insistently as if there was a young calf in there. Very perplexing indeed, the humpback thought to herself.

❧ 20 ❧

The directors of the Textran Corporation sat in their boardroom in a Manhattan tower. They were putting finishing touches to the plan which would bring in the cash they needed to avert catastrophe—a threatened takeover.

The move would also enable the corporation to take advantage of a lucrative investment opportunity in the Amazon.

The seven board members were well-dressed and well-groomed. They exuded intelligence, confidence, and charm. They even, for the most part, exuded health—although it was the kind more associated with fitness centers than with woods or mountains.

They were good people, every one of them. If questioned, they would all have acknowledged it. They would have pointed out they were simply doing what was good for the company, for their families, their careers, the economy, and so on.

In their lofty tower in the heart of New York City, well insulated against inconveniences such as wind, rain, and sun, and divorced from any sense of the needs or vital role of the natural world, the seven met and made their decree. They exercised their feudal authority over the earth.

The subject they had been considering together for the past hour or so was redwoods; specifically, a redwood grove in northern California owned by a small family lumber company. The company had practiced selective logging in the area for nearly half a century but was being forced out of business by mounting debt.

Textran had an option to purchase this desirable asset.

The redwoods were there for the taking. They were a fortune waiting to be plucked.

"There is enough timber in that grove," observed one of the board members enthusiastically, "to get this corporation out of trouble and guarantee growth for the next three to five years." He paused, adding for the sake of one or two hesitant colleagues, "Let's be realistic for Chrissakes. The redwoods are doomed anyway. Someone is going to cut down those trees—why not us? Why should we deprive ourselves?"

They had heard the argument before, of course, the hesitant ones. Each time they heard it, however, it sounded a little more reasonable. The need for expediency seemed a little more obvious. The well-being of the entire corporation was, after all, at stake.

The vote, when it came, was unanimous: to proceed with the immediate acquisition of the Littleton Timber Co., of Littleton, California, with a view to clear-cutting their stands of old growth redwood.

❧ 21 ❧

The man was sitting in a coffee shop waiting to cover a story for his newspaper when the old feelings of loneliness and frustration returned.

Perhaps he had been thinking too much about his ex-wife, Jennifer. In any case, there they were. They burst in and surrounded him like a gang of young hoodlums out for mischief.

"Lonely these days, huh?" the leader of the hoodlums said with a leer, winking at his friends. "No one to keep you company but your cat. Sleeping alone every night, huh?" The hoodlums sniggered among themselves and the leader took a step forward. He stuck his jaw out belligerently.

"Might as well admit it, meathead. Your life is a screwup, a walking disaster. You know why she left? It's because you're such a useless sonofabitch and always have been."

The hoodlums laughed uproariously. Then they began making fun of the novel he was writing about Vietnam. They told him it was a waste of time and he had bitten off more than he could chew. They told him he would never even get it finished.

"You know what?" said the ringleader with a sneer. "Even if you do finish it no one will want to read it."

They tore his would-be novel to pieces. They mashed it into the ground.

They laughed at the time he had spent with the redwood, ridiculing the notion that anything important had occurred. "Haven't you figured it out yet? It was all your imagination," said one of the vandals with a pitying look. "Boy, you are out to lunch."

They reminded the man how he had never been able to talk with his father, even when his father lay dying.

"What a mess you're in," the ringleader went on. "You should have gone ahead and shot yourself. Do you really think you're going to do anything worthwhile in your life?

"How stupid can you get? You're going to end up helpless and decrepit like your father and then you will die the same as everyone else. As for this dream about meeting the right woman, forget it. The whole idea is a load of crap—it's a fairy story for kids."

The painful memories were still rising up inside him but the man did not care.

The demons were still shooting their mouths off but he wasn't listening.

He was thinking about the redwood and how strong and proud it stood, reaching up to the heavens. He was remembering the sigh of the wind in the forest. He was hearing again the murmur of the creek.

"Be still, my heart," he said simply. "Everything is going to be all right."

In the goodness of time, the man thought to himself, whatever needed to happen in his life would happen. Whatever fulfillment was right for him would come.

There was stillness in his soul. There was peace in his heart. He felt at one with the universe. As he sat solitary but not alone in the coffee shop the man blazed with happiness.

22

The woman drank deep from an invisible chalice of bliss during her time in the hospital, the memory of her visit to the realm of light so strong there was scarcely room in her thoughts for anything else.

"If only I had your secret, dear," said an old man, suffering from a terminal illness, who felt the peace in the woman and looked for every opportunity to be with her.

Little by little, though, as she returned to the details and contradictions of everyday life, she realized that the glorious sense of freedom and expanded selfhood she had touched during her near-death experience was only a step—albeit a profound and significant one—in her life's journey.

There were still challenges to meet. There were still fears and uncertainties. Sadness still tore at her heart, sometimes more intensely than ever before. At times she felt that the earth—her own body, specifically—was a prison preventing the full expression of herself.

Nonetheless, her near-death experience had wrought powerful changes. It had transformed her whole way of thinking—her attitudes, her values.

She was not so anxious or worried about her career, for example—the endless pursuit of fame and fortune—as she once had been. This was brought home to her forcibly one day when she received a telephone call from her agent telling her that she had failed to get the part in the new movie which she had coveted. It had gone to Lia Marelli after all.

Two months earlier, the news would have devastated her. She would have been very emotional. She would have been swearing. Her agent feared such a reaction, she could tell. It was obvious in the careful way he tried to break the news. He was concerned—worried for her.

Her breath did catch in her throat. She let out a cry. But she was surprised how steady she felt.

"C'est la vie," she said, after a pause. "It's not really a surprise, Carl. I thought it might go this way. Please don't feel badly."

When she had hung up, she wondered if she had been too philosophical. She didn't want Carl to think she was losing her commitment to her career.

Her work was still important to her, but it wasn't an obsession anymore. It wasn't a matter of life or death, as it had been once upon a time.

Part of the reason, no doubt, she thought to herself, was that other priorities had emerged into her consciousness. She had become very concerned about ecology, and she read a lot about the threats facing the environment. She had a deeper love for nature—and for her fellow human beings.

While this heightened sensitivity to what was around her sometimes brought its pleasure, and fulfillment, sometimes it brought the sharpest pain. When she saw a man slap a small boy across the face in a parking lot for some minor misbehavior she felt the assault so keenly she gasped aloud. She wanted to go to the boy and comfort him, perhaps speak to the man. But she knew there was nothing she could do. She had seen the anger in the father's eyes. She had sensed his underlying frustration and resentment toward life. "Why do people have to be so mean," the woman wondered sadly. "Why don't they realize the peace that is within them."

Although she knew she had lost her fear of death, other uncertainties loomed large at times—for instance, she worried that her life was moving in a way that was out of her control.

"If only one of my friends had been through something like this," she thought sometimes. "We could sit down and talk about it, and it would help me see where I am going."

But this was not the case. In fact she gave up trying to discuss the deeper things of life—particularly her own experience—with other people, because it tended to create difficulties and misunderstanding. She was aware that some of her friends and acquaintances had distanced themselves from her, and this, too, brought pain.

In quiet moments the woman knew that all that had happened to her was good. "The unknown is not really a difficult or frightening place," she would think, remembering her wonderful journey through the tunnel of light. Nonetheless she longed for a sign—some external indication of where her life was headed, or what her next step should be.

It was on a warm August night two or three weeks after the phone call from her agent that she dreamed about the whale.

She dreamed she had gone to the seashore and was swimming in the clear turquoise ocean when she began to tire. She wanted to swim back to shore but could not. She grew weaker and weaker, and slipped beneath the waves. As she struggled to save herself she heard a strange, magical cry. She saw a whale, huge, black, with glistening skin and a tiny nub of dorsal fin on its back. The whale swam close—so close she could have touched it—and looked directly at her. There was such love in the creature's gaze that she lost all her fear. The whale glided beneath her and lifted her gently to the surface of the sea. Then it carried her on its back to shore, steering itself with long, scalloped flippers. The appendages were white on their edges and looked like angel's wings.

The woman awoke with the sound of the whale's cry echoing in her head.

≈ 23 ≈

The sun, of course, had never failed in its love. Every day for twenty-seven-hundred years it had poured out its radiance, that the redwood might be strengthened and sustained.

The rain still came, and the wind, and the sea mists.

The earth still gave of her bounty.

However, there was one thing missing from the symphony of life of which the redwood was a part, and that was the love of humankind.

The human heart had been torn out of the forest the previous century. It disappeared when the white man came and began to harass and murder the first people. Ever since, the redwood and its kind had experienced pangs of loneliness such as had never been known before.

For thousands of years, while the people of the forest lived along this coast, the redwood trees were honored. They played a part in the spiritual life of the people—and in their material life, too, as from time to time, with elk-horn wedges and adzes made from mussel shells, they cut planks from fallen or driftwood logs to build their homes. Living trees, of course, were rarely touched.

It had been a long time since men ran through the redwood groves, swift, silent, traveling like the wind, their deep breaths a nourishment and blessing.

Perhaps this was why the redwood remembered with something close to yearning the man who three times now had come to sit down beside it, and run his hands over its skin, so that the tree felt refreshed.

But it was not only loneliness for human beings that the redwood was feeling on this particular day.

There was something else. The tree was not sure, but it sensed that its time on earth might be drawing to a close. The tick, tick, tick of the little drum in the god's hand seemed to be getting louder. It seemed to be coming closer.

The tree had survived so much in its long life. Eight times it had been attacked by fire, the worst being in 503AD when a blaze nearly penetrated the heartwood. In response to that near-killing burn the tree had immediately begun to build a buttress to give it greater strength and help it remain upright.

Besides the fires there had been floods, when the creek—normally so gentle—turned into a raging torrent that threatened the redwood's very foundation.

All these dangers and more the tree had faced. But there was one thing it could not overcome. It could not survive the greed and foolishness of modern man.

≈ 24 ≈

It was a chance remark by a male friend that made the woman decide to see the clairvoyant. The friend was impressed with how accurately the clairvoyant described some aspects of his nature and things that had happened in his life.

The woman pushed the buzzer beside the gaily painted yellow door of the house.

"It is good that my father cannot see me now," she thought as she waited on the doorstep. "He would turn over in his grave."

"Monique Dumont," said the clairvoyant as she came to the door. "What a pleasure to meet you in person. I have always loved your movies. Please come this way."

They sat down. A scarlet cloth covered the table, which was bare except for a single lighted candle and a crystal. The clairvoyant picked up the crystal and held it in her hands and went into a silence.

"The crystal helps me to tune into your vibrations," she said after a few minutes. She looked up and smiled. "This is a most interesting dream you have been having," she continued, "about meeting the whale. I cannot see any details, however—perhaps you could describe it to me?"

The actress gasped. How could the clairvoyant know about the dream? She realized that this attractive young woman was perceptive indeed. She began to describe the dream—how she was about to drown, and a whale rose up beneath her and carried her to shore. She described the magical cry of the whale.

There was calm on the clairvoyant's face as she listened, and she stroked the crystal. After another long pause the clairvoyant began to speak.

"You have something unique to offer into the well-being of the planet," she said quietly. "Of that there is no question." A wonderful smile illuminated her face and gave comfort to the actress.

"You have been through many difficult experiences in the past year, and have sometimes wondered for your sanity. I see that you had a nasty automobile accident and that you had an experience of seeing beyond the veil at that time.

"All this confusion and inner conflict has come because the truth of yourself is rising up from your own depths, demanding to be recognized. You have not known what to do about this. For a while you did your best to ignore it and suppress it, but of course it would not go away."

Again the clairvoyant smiled her brilliant smile.

"The dream is telling you to trust what is coming up from inside yourself in this way even though it may be painful or confusing. The dream is also a reminder that there is a place deep inside yourself where you hold all the answers you need to come clear and claim your destiny."

The actress nodded her head. Her large brown eyes had softened. It was so wonderful to be with someone who understood. "Mais oui," she exclaimed. "I understand. But the whale. Why the whale?"

The clairvoyant walked over to a bookshelf and returned with a book, which she opened and laid on the table.

"This is a picture of a petroglyph," said the clairvoyant quietly. "These ancient rock carvings say that there was a time when the Earth shifted and Lemuria, the motherland, sank below the waves. The symbols show how the red race fled to North America from the west and crossed many rivers and mountains. They were searching for solid ground as the waters receded.

"It is said that whales saw all these events and have kept the records and knowledge of the motherland alive. If this is true then the secrets of all the ages are contained within their memory—which is why their calls have such magic for some people."

The clairvoyant looked up from her crystal. Her eyes gleamed with intensity.

"I believe your life is entwined with that of the whales," she said. "It may be that part of your task is to help others to love these creatures—and understand the gift they bring."

Again there was a silence.

The actress started to ask another question but then hesitated.

The clairvoyant laid down the crystal. "You are forty years old and you wonder if you are ever going to find a lasting and satisfying relationship with a man," she said, smiling.

"I think it is very likely. In fact I believe you may meet such a person fairly soon. I am not sure how, but I sense that it could happen, and that it could be an important step in fulfilling your destiny."

≈ 25 ≈

The two urges competed with each other as the humpback swam south with her calf after the summer feasting in the Gulf of Alaska.

"They are so opposite—so very different," the whale thought to herself.

There was the urge that was familiar to her, the traditional compulsion which she and her kind had followed for hundreds and thousands of years; the urge, after the annual feeding, to swim south to warm waters for mating and breeding.

And there was this other urge, not safe or familiar at all—the strange new idea that had crept quietly into her consciousness over the past few months, to be with humans and commune with them.

The humpback looked with pride at her calf, swimming strongly forty or fifty feet away. He had done well, she thought contentedly. He was a fine calf, no doubt about it. In fact after eleven months of constant care, she had now virtually weaned him. He was ready to fend for himself. He had filled out nicely in the northern waters, and was much wiser in the ways of the sea. Although a little slow in some respects—obstinate was a better word—on the whole he had been a good learner.

Yes, he has done well, the humpback decided.

"If necessary, if I decide to pursue this strange endeavor, my calf will be able to continue with the others," she thought. "He will find his way alright, and his 'aunties' will keep an eye on him, too."

And yet the urge to mate—perhaps to conceive again—was strong, etched deep into her very cells. What was she going to do anyway, even if she did swim to Turtle Island, the land of the humans? When she thought about it logically, there was no sense to the idea at all. Common sense said, "Don't be foolish. Keep going with the others. Stay with your own kind."

Sometimes, when she awoke from a nap, and before she got into her swimming rhythm, she was sure that the idea of diverting to the coast where the humans lived was ridiculous. Totally unacceptable.

But once she was on the move and the power of life was pulsing through her and she heard the waves and wind beating above her head, the doubts disappeared.

"Remember too," the whale said to herself one day as the pod swam in heavy seas about one hundred miles west of the northern California coast, "that it is only for a few days. After I have visited with the humans, I will still be able to rejoin the others in the south."

The hardest part, once she had made up her mind to turn toward land, was to handle the initial confusion and fright of her calf when she shared her intent with him. Gently, over two or three days, she explained what she planned to do. She said it would not be right to take him along, and he was capable of looking after himself now. She pointed out that she would be rejoining the herd soon in any case, and that of course the other mothers would keep an eye on him. She had never been so proud in her life when the calf, at a certain point, understood and accepted her decision. The two rubbed against each other and caressed with their flippers. With a farewell to the other humpbacks in the group the mother whale turned and began swimming toward the distant shore.

"Is it really the right thing?" she asked herself anxiously. But something inside urged her on. She felt a current of excitement greater than she had ever known before.

"Are you there, redwood?" she asked, many hours later, as the water began to change color and she knew that land was close. A wind was blowing hard behind her from the west, and for a while she enjoyed traveling on the surface and planing upon the waves which the wind made.

The whale saw a small group of terns flit by, with their distinctive black caps and white bodies. For a few minutes a lone petrel flew along on top of the driving scud as if enjoying her company, before looping off to the south. But on the whole there was not much other life, either under the surface of the sea or above it; certainly not as much as when she was young.

"I am following my urge, redwood," said the whale aloud. "I am coming in to shore, so that I may meet some humans and commune with them."

But her friend, she presumed, was asleep, or busy, for there was no answer at all.

As she soared upon the crests of the waves, the humpback was also traveling in her memory. Back, she went, and back, and back, exploring the ancient records of her kind stored deep in the secret vaults of her being....

She was back in a time of innocence when there was no such thing as disease or death and the faces of men and women shone with understanding and they were able to communicate with the animals and ascend into heaven at will.

She was back in the original paradisiacal home that the Sumerians called Dilmun, where Adapa, the first human, lived with honor and uprightness.

She was back in the Golden Age of Cronos, when all living things were gentle and obedient in their love for the universal law of life.

She was back before the dawn of religion, before the era of politics. It was like it was on the other side of a dark veil—the peace and happiness of that time when creatures and humans lived in harmony together.

❧ 26 ❧

The flame shimmered and danced. It was the fire of love and it was burning away the misconceptions that had kept the man confused and afraid.

It was dissolving the veil that had kept him separated from his own true self—the light within him.

He was beginning to realize that he did not need to wait for other people to change or for his circumstances to improve—the opportunity to express his own selfhood was always present, and when he did this it brought its own change, and its own freedom.

He was beginning to think that his depression was not a curse visited upon him by a callous, meaningless god—it was an opportunity to develop a new understanding and approach to his life.

"I suspect the old idea of progress is all wrong," he wrote in his journal one day, underlining the word 'wrong' three times. "Not only does it usually mean denuding or damaging the environment. It often over-looks the fact that a person or society is already signifi-cant, in the sense that the opportunity to express love is immediately present with everyone."

To express the love that was in him, he now believed, was the most significant thing he could do.

In him was light.

In him was the power to bring change.

One day the man decided to go to the zoo. As he walked around he became more and more disturbed at the sight of the beautiful animals imprisoned in confined areas. Feelings of resentment began to rise up and trouble him.

"Wait a minute," the man said to himself. "What is going on here? Am I so helpless that I have nothing to offer into this situation?"

The answer came to him as he stood by a glass window at the aquarium, watching a beluga whale swim round and round in the tank.

"I will invite the beluga to come and play with me," said the man, and that is what he did—silently, because there were a few people walking back and forth.

Much to his surprise, the whale seemed to hear the invitation. It swam over and looked through the glass near where he was standing.

The man put his eye to the window also and they stared at each other for a few moments.

"I think he is smiling at me," the man thought with amazement. "I will try something else."

He forgot there were people around and moved quickly sideways about half-a-dozen steps. The whale followed him. He danced in the other direction; again the whale followed. More people began to gather and watch. Some laughed at the fun of it.

The man thought for a moment then stepped back and began turning in a series of circles. The whale immediately began swimming in circles.

Ten minutes went by. The man was happy and refreshed—and the other people too, who had been watching. As the man waved goodbye to the beluga and turned to leave he noticed an attractive, dark-haired woman looking at him. There was a smile on her face and she had obviously been enjoying the interplay with the whale. She looked familiar for some reason although he did not know why. The man smiled back as he passed the woman and headed toward the exit.

❧ 27 ❧

A day or two after his visit to the zoo the man was eating lunch with a fellow reporter in a bar. He had ordered a steak sandwich and a beer.

"I wonder if I will ever find a woman who is right for me?" the man thought during an idle moment. "How strange it would be if she is out there right now—maybe having exactly the same thoughts as I am. It's possible, isn't it? It's possible."

What would she look like, the man wondered, indulging himself further. It was then that he remembered the tall, dark-haired woman with the gorgeous brown eyes—somewhere in her late thirties, he guessed—who had been watching as he played with the beluga. Was it his imagination, or had there been a hint of mutual understanding between them as he turned and left the scene?

Something clicked in his memory and he knew who the woman was. "Monique Dumont," he said to himself in surprise. "Of course. That's who it was. I thought I had seen her somewhere before."

It was time to get back to the office. The man paid his bill, laughing at a joke his friend had shared. But the woman kept coming back into his thoughts.

One Saturday morning he was working at home on his novel. The book was going well, and he dared to think he would finish it soon. His cat dozed in one of her favorite spots—on top of his desk—in fact on top of a stack of recently completed chapters.

For some reason the man came to an abrupt stop in mid-paragraph, and his thoughts turned toward the redwood. He felt a wave of inexplicable sadness and loneliness.

"I haven't been to see the redwood for quite a while," he thought to himself, wondering why he felt like he did, and where the sense of foreboding was coming from.

He decided to visit the redwood grove as soon as he could.

≋ 28 ≋

The humpback whale swam under the bridge into the harbor in the early afternoon, even as her calf continued with the rest of the pod to their summer breeding grounds off the coast of Mexico.

Her arrival was the biggest story on the local news and it wasn't long before it captured the imagination of the nation.

Why the whale swam into the harbor no one, of course, knew, although there were various conjectures. The whale was afflicted with parasites that caused aberrations in its brain, some marine biologists supposed. The whale had been confused by naval electronic signaling. The whale had a screw loose—or more likely, as one TV anchor said with a chuckle, a flipper.

Nor did the experts know the sex of the whale; there was no way to find that out except by examining its underside, which was hardly a practical proposition. For some reason or another—probably a local newscaster started the trend—it was agreed that the whale was female, and she was named "Helga the humpback."

As she swam across the harbor, "Helga" felt enormous tremors of excitement moving through her. She could feel the presence of the humans, the energy that had drawn her upon this improbable adventure. Passing beneath another bridge, she stopped to frolic for half-an-hour. She breached twice, leaping high out of the water and arcing her body as she fell with a mighty crash onto the surface of the bay. She swam in circles, from time to time lifting one of her flippers as if to wave at the spectators. All in all she showed off shamelessly for the excited people who gathered in increasing numbers to watch. Some of the humans came in boats, while others stood on shore or lined the bridge. There were cheers and shouts. There was the honking of horns.

Other sounds began to be added. A number of small naval boats arrived. The crews began clanging pipes together underwater, trying to shepherd the whale back toward the sea.

But the humpback had not come this far to turn around and leave immediately.

She calmly ignored the clangings of the pipes. When she had finished her play, she nosed into a creek leading off the harbor. As she was moving leisurely up the channel she ran aground on a mud flat, beside rocks that bore a No Trespassing sign.

29

The woman caught her first glimpse of the humpback when she turned on the news. The report said the Coast Guard and other authorities were doing their best to help the whale get back to sea.

"Bon dieu," she said, gazing incredulously at the screen. "Une grande baleine."

Although she was only seeing an image on a screen, the wonder of a whale coming right into the city entranced her. She sat in awe as the event unfolded on her TV. She knew instinctively that the event was related to her dream.

It was just past midday. She determined to drive north immediately after lunch to see the whale.

❧ **30** ❧

The man stood by the stump of the fallen redwood. He looked at the carnage around him and tried to deal with the anger pounding in his chest, and the pain tearing at his heart.

It looked like a picture he had seen of a First World War battlefield in Flanders. It looked like a scene from hell.

The land, once a forest, a sanctuary, fertile, alive, home to so many kinds of animals and plants and birds, was now a wasteland of stumps and debris. Here and there a few spindly trees had escaped destruction—gaunt survivors of the holocaust. Skidders had scarred and gouged the soil where once the earth, like a fruitful woman, succored and empowered her growing things. But now the earth was mute. She trembled in the aftermath of rape.

The man looked down at the barren bleeding stump—twelve feet across—which was all that remained of the redwood.

He looked up, high, high above him, where once the redwood had soared into the vaulted azure sky and communed with the sun. All that met his eyes was the gaping emptiness of space.

"You were too tall and proud. They had to reduce you to their own pygmy level," the man thought bitterly. He took out a handkerchief and wiped his eyes.

He sat down beside the stump. What was he to do? What could he do? They all came trooping in, the feelings of anger and frustration, hopelessness and fear; in all their power they came, the demons that had beset him at various times in his life.

"What hope is there for Nature," the man thought despairingly, "as long as people behave like this? It's all going to go, just like the redwood, and there's nothing I or anyone else can do about it. The forces of destruction are too strong. They are too entrenched."

He sat silently for a long time; there was no life around him except for a few small ants. He watched as they crawled over his pant legs and disappeared, a lonely brigade intent upon their business, into the brush.

The man laid a hand on the bark of the stump. He felt nothing; no life, no pulse, no magic. Hating his feelings of hopelessness, he got up and walked around. He looked back at the spot where the redwood had stood. He looked at the vacancy that extended around him in every direction.

No life, no pulse, no magic.

Nothing.

The man could not help himself. A cry of outrage and despair rose from deep in his soul and hung quivering upon the still air.

Quivering, and unanswered.

〜 **31** 〜

The humpback whale was beached on a mud flat close
to shore. Rescuers were busy tossing water on her massive
body to keep her from dehydrating.

They were using pumps, buckets, and towels, and they
had been at it all day. Other workers and volunteers,
including marine biologists, veterinarians, and the Coast
Guard, were assembling a harness and more gear in a bid
to tow the whale free of the flat once the tide began to rise.

One of the Coast Guard men, a freckle-faced, fair-
haired youngster, recognized the woman and grinned at
her. "Hi," he said. "Excuse me, but aren't you Monique
Dumont?"

The woman smiled back. "Yes I am," she replied. "Will
you be able to free the whale?"

"We'll free her alright—just hope she doesn't get stuck
again someplace else." The youngster hesitated.

"Miss Dumont," he said, a little shy. "Could I get your
autograph please? For my kid brother?"

The woman smiled again, and signed her name. She
picked up a bucket and scooped water on the stranded
whale.

The creature was like a being from another planet, she
thought. So huge. So magnificent. She walked beside the
45-foot long body toward the whale's head and saw that

its eyes were closed. She stood, absorbing the humpback's beauty and power, and yet sad at its present helplessness.

"You beautiful creature," she said softly, under her breath. "Hello."

The whale opened a tiny eye about the size of an orange and looked directly at her. An electric current shot through the woman. They stared at each other.

"You are so beautiful," said the woman softly. "So beautiful!" She reached out and gently touched the smooth, sheeny black skin that the workers were trying so hard to keep moist. She felt the creature tremble—she felt energy pulse back and forth through her fingers.

"I know you," she thought. "And you know me. Mon dieu, we know each other."

The woman continued gently stroking the whale. The creature looked at her with an expression that was inquisitive, quizzical, and wise. Was it her imagination? She thought she saw a gleam of humor too.

"You know much, dear whale," said the woman. "Are you the one who has been in my dreams?" As if she had heard the question, the humpback suddenly uttered a low, deep cry that was music to the woman's soul.

Monique Dumont was ecstatic. Something healed in her heart. She felt a veil of separation dissolve.

Life is one, she thought. She determined, in that instant, to do all she could to increase love and understanding between humans and the wild whales.

She tossed more water over the parched skin.

"Thank you for coming, great whale," she said. "I will always love you."

Once more she touched the smooth black skin that was drying and fissuring in the sun, and which they had to get back into its proper element. She touched one of the barnacles that grew in a starlike cluster on the whale's chin.

The tide had been rising little by little. An air compressor unit had been brought in and the man who was leading the rescue operation directed its placement. A pump began to suck mud from beneath the humpback.

"We'll do our best to help her but she's stuck on the bottom by suction," the team leader said. "She's going to have to put some effort into it herself if she's going to get free."

As if the humpback heard the man's words she wriggled in the mud, flipping her fins and raising her tail a few times. The woman loved to see the whale move.

Amidst the busyness of the rescue scene the woman had a surprising thought.

"It is not we who are rescuing you," she murmured to herself. "It is you who have come to rescue us. You have come to lead us away from our ignorance, and show us how separate we have been from the creatures of the sea, and from the wholeness of life."

"Go," said the woman. "Go, dear friend, back into your element. But remember, I will always be with you."

The rescue workers and the crowd standing further back on the shore were cheering and shouting. Horns honked. People clapped and sang. Some held hands.

Presently, with some mighty heaves, the humpback flipped herself off the mud flat and into the channel.

The woman watched with tears in her eyes as the whale began to swim clear. With effortless ease and grace she swam, while a flotilla of boats followed, trying to guide her toward the sea.

❧ 32 ❧

The lord of all life was there when the woman opened her heart to the whale. The god felt the man's passionate grief for the fallen redwood.

"The veil of separation on earth is thinning," the god observed.

"It is because the flame is growing hotter," said the jewel-eyed one who danced with him. "It is compelling change everywhere."

They breathed together upon the flame that the god carried in his hand.

"We must keep it that way," he replied.

33

The humpback whale spent a week cruising the waters of the harbor and exploring the channels that led off it. With each day she became more and more of a national celebrity, and people realized how much they loved whales and cared about them.

"It is working out better than I could possibly have imagined," the whale thought contentedly one day as she sunned herself in a protected cove; occasionally she raised a flipper to the busloads of tourists and whale watchers lining the shore and nearby bridge.

Once again the humpback tried to engage the redwood in conversation. The tree had been silent for several days and the humpback was worried.

"Are you there, redwood?" asked the whale. "You would never believe the time I am having.

"All kinds of people have been coming to see me—I never believed humans could be so friendly." The whale paused, and did a dive so as to cool off. She spouted a fine column of spray twenty feet into the air as she surfaced again.

"But the most exciting thing of all," the whale continued, resuming her sunbathing, "was when I met this woman. It was the communion I had been longing for, although I did not realize what it was I was seeking. We just kept looking at each other and when she touched me it was like we had always been friends—like there had never been any separation between us.

"I think that something is happening, redwood. Humans really are beginning to change and be our friends."

There was no reply.

"Redwood?" the whale beseeched.

"Redwood, please speak to me. Are you there?"

Grief pierced the heart of the humpback. It was as if she knew now that the tree was no longer alive, was no longer standing upright and magnificent in its protected place near the sea.

"Dear redwood," the whale exclaimed. "You have been such a wonderful friend. How I shall miss you if, indeed, you do not exist any more. You have brought so much strength and assurance into my life; I shall never forget you, dear friend."

The whale thought about things and decided her mission was probably finished. It was time to continue her journey south and join the other humpbacks.

A flotilla of upwards of 40 motor boats had been gathering in the distance—some of them civilian and some military—and the whale watched as they began to move toward her.

The flotilla began to shepherd the humpback toward the open sea. Another boat had appeared in front of her and was leading the way. The most wonderful flutelike sounds echoed from this lead boat. They were the sounds of humpback whales feeding and socializing; the sounds were being broadcast over a submerged loudspeaker system.

As she listened to the familiar cries and chatter the humpback felt her body quicken and she longed to be at sea with her own kind again.

She followed the flutelike sounds.

❧ 34 ❧

The man was stiff, sore, and cold from lying on the hard ground. He had slept—although poorly—amid the ruins of the forest. All night he lay beside the redwood stump, keeping warm as best he could with the blanket he fetched from his car. All night he kept the vigil for his departed friend, just as many years previously, in the paddy fields and jungles of Vietnam, he sometimes kept a vigil for human comrades who had fallen.

The air was crisp and clear, with a tang from the sea. But it did not lift the spirits of the man as he stood, rubbing the sleep from his eyes, gazing once again at the stump of the tree and the wasteland around him.

What was this nudge he felt? As if a small voice was trying to get his attention?

Something made him bend down and look more closely at the base of the fallen redwood.

He knelt on the ground.

Nudging up through the barren wreckage was an incredible sight. A tiny redwood shoot was growing from the base of the tree. The man cleared away some debris so that he could see the miracle more clearly.

Perhaps it was the spirit of the tiny redwood that told him.

Perhaps it was the truth within himself.

Perhaps it was the spirit of the whole throbbing universe that spoke with the man.

But in any case he knew. It was seared irrevocably into his soul that nothing that humans did, nothing, would ultimately prevail over Nature, or over the planet, or over the wholeness of which the planet is a part.

Life was too powerful.

Nature, the elements, the Earth, the solar system, the universe beyond—these things were too strong.

"They are in league together and they will not be destroyed," the man thought. "If worst came to worst, it will be humans—not Nature—who are sloughed off the skin of the planet."

But perhaps that need not be, he murmured to himself.

There were many men and women of good will in the world.

Perhaps all that was needed—it was all he could do anyway—was to play his own part in the wholeness that he had come to sense and know through his friendship with the redwood.

"One way I can make a difference is through my writing," he thought. He would do some research. He would write articles and stories about the natural world and care of the environment. Ben might let him start a column; he could write a book ...

He felt the resentment that had been building up inside him like a volcano begin to release.

He felt a new sense of purpose taking shape in his mind.

The man stood in the midst of the desolate clearing where it seemed life had been so rudely extinguished—he knew now that it was alive still—and put his hands on top of the redwood stump. He smelt the fragrance that came from the severed trunk even in death.

"I shall carry on your work, great tree," he said quietly.

"It shall be my endeavor to be as useful and upright as you were, to play my part in the song of creation even as you did for so many centuries."

The man paused, hearing again the internal stillness which he felt so powerfully when he first came to the redwood forest.

He put his finger in his mouth, tasted the stickiness of the redwood. He picked up a cup-sized piece of bark that was lying on the ground and put it in his pocket. It would be a reminder of his friend who had died, yet still lived in his heart.

❦ 35 ❦

It was late in the afternoon. They met in a bookshop on 14th Street, although if it hadn't happened there, it would probably have happened somewhere else. The woman had gone in to buy a book about whales. The man didn't have a reason: he was walking past the shop on his way to a restaurant and an impulse drew him in.

He was idly scanning a shelf of new releases when he saw the dark-haired woman whom he had noticed at the zoo when he was having fun with the beluga. It was the actress, Monique Dumont.

The man did not allow himself to hesitate. He walked straight down the aisle to where the woman was leafing through a large book. He noticed that it contained pictures of whales.

"Hello," said the man, a grin lifting the corners of his wide mouth. "I don't know if you'll remember me, but I saw you at the zoo some time back—at the aquarium—I was making a fool of myself with the beluga."

The woman looked up.

"Yes, I remember you," she said with a captivating little smile. "I remember you well. I enjoyed your dance with the whale."

The man was not pushy by nature and had felt uncomfortable approaching the woman. But when he saw she was at ease—and obviously friendly—he began to relax.

"I'm John Bratton," he said. "Talking of whales, I'm sure you've seen Helga, like everyone else in California?"

The woman laughed. It was a warm, throaty sound.

"But of course. Wasn't she wonderful? I felt so close to her—I never experienced such deep communion with a wild creature before."

"It looks like you're buying a book about whales," the man noted.

"Yes, I have to learn all I can about them."

The man paused, feeling embarrassed again. "You're Monique Dumont, aren't you. I thought your face was familiar when I saw you at the aquarium."

"That's right," the woman smiled. "And who are you, Mr. Bratton, if I may ask?"

"I'm a reporter," he replied. "I work for the *State Register*." His inhibitions were still trying to get the better of him. Oh go away, he said to them firmly.

"Forgive me for being brash," the man continued, a warm but determined smile on his face. "But I wonder if you would join me for dinner? There's a charming little French place close by—I was just on my way there as a matter of fact."

The woman looked at him intently. She saw the pain etched into his face. She saw the strength that had endured the pain. In the place of knowing deep in a woman's heart she felt his trustworthiness.

"Amazing," she thought. "It is actually happening— just as the clairvoyant said it might."

"You are very kind," she said, her velvet brown eyes dancing. "I would be delighted ... French cuisine too, you said."

She walked over to the counter and paid for the book.

"Shall we go?" she said to the man. A smile shimmered between them like sunlight dancing upon the sea.

❧❧ 36 ❧❧

The conversation flowed irrepressibly between them. There seemed to be so much to talk about. It was as if they had known each other forever but were behind on one another's news. Not until the coffee arrived did they pause and become quiet, sensing a need to be still.

Even the stillness was alive, though. It sparkled like dew on a flower. It sparkled like a mountain stream.

Finally the man began to tell the woman about the redwood and the beauty and strength it had brought into his life. He described how he had stood beside the stump of the fallen tree and resolved to do all he could to be a connector between the natural world and humankind—to live usefully and with honor from his own true source, just as the tree had done. He saw that the woman understood what he was trying to say, and he was glad.

The woman told about her depression and the automobile accident. She told how the accident had opened her eyes to a different world—a world of unimaginable beauty and light.

A tear coursed down the woman's cheek.

"There must be other women out there going through all kinds of hell and thinking they are alone, just like I did," she continued.

Her voice began to quiver. Her hand played with a napkin. She looked down at the table.

"I want to help them," she said. "I want to tell them that it is alright to go into the darkness because on the other side there is light."

The woman looked up. Her eyes softened. "There is something else I want to do, too," she said. "I want to help the whales. I want to use whatever fame or money I have to help people understand them better."

The flame that was leaping between them burned hotter. It bore exquisite hues and shapes visible to no one else in the restaurant but visible to them. Time ceased. They could not even hear the little drum that goes tick, tick, tick and veils the presence of eternity.

They were one in the radiance of the lord of life, and his queen.

They were one in the flame of love.